RAIN & SHINE

RAIN & SHINE

STORIES BY

Paul Rogers

Illustrated by Chris Burke

ORCHARD BOOKS

A division of Franklin Watts, Inc.

NEW YORK

For my children

Text copyright © 1987 by Paul Rogers
Illustrations copyright © 1987 by Chris Burke
FIRST AMERICAN EDITION 1988

Orchard Books
387 Park Avenue South
New York, New York 10016

Orchard Books Canada
20 Torbay Road
Markham, Ontario 23P 1G6

Orchard Books is a division of Franklin Watts, Inc.

MANUFACTURED IN THE UNITED STATES OF AMERICA

Book design by Tere LoPrete

10   9   8   7   6   5   4   3   2   1

The text of this book is set in 14 pt. Janson
The illustrations are line

Library of Congress Cataloging-in-Publication Data
Rogers, Paul, 1950-
    Rain and shine / Paul Rogers ; illustrated by Chris Burke. — 1st
American ed.
        p.   cm.
    Summary: Presents seven episodes in the busy lives of seven-year-
old Ned and his younger brother and sister, who play hide and seek,
make spider pies, and enjoy an imaginary playmate.
    ISBN 0-531-08371-3 (lib. bdg.).   ISBN 0-531-05771-2
    [1. Brothers and sisters—Fiction.]   I. Burke, Chris, ill.
II. Title.
PZ7.R6257Rai   1988
[E]—dc19
                                                88-1453
                                                    CIP
                                                    AC

Contents

RAIN & SHINE

Before You Begin

The stories in this book are about three children.

Ned is seven.

His sister Nina is four and a half.

And their little brother Joshy is just two.

They live in a house in the country with their Mom and Dad and a big dog called Acorn and a stripy cat called Tinker.

Joshy's Spoon

Ned flung open his curtains and the sun flooded in. This day, he decided, they were going to be pirates. So he put on his eye patch and went down to breakfast.

Nina and Joshy were already at the table. "We're going to be pirates today," he told them.

Joshy didn't mind what he was. He was concentrating on eating. Between the bowl and his mouth anything could happen. The spoon could lose its load, drop to the floor, or even if it got safely to him, it could miss his mouth and end up leaving the food stuck to some remote part of his face.

Nina said she'd be a pirate, but only if she could have an eye patch too. So Ned made her one with cardboard and a rubber band. When she put it on, though, she said she couldn't see where she was going, so she ended up sliding it to one side. Ned thought she looked silly—who ever heard of a pirate with an ear patch?—but he didn't argue because the ship was waiting. As soon as Joshy had had his face and hands wiped, they went outside and set sail.

"Where are we going?" asked Nina.

"To the treasure island, of course," said Ned finding a stick that would do for a telescope.

"Are we there?" she asked.

"Not yet," he said. Then suddenly, looking down his stick, he shouted, "Land ahoy!"

"Let me see!" said Nina.

But just at that moment Joshy fell overboard. Without fear, Ned leaped into the raging sea. But Joshy didn't want to be saved. In fact, he didn't want to be a pirate either. He'd found a caterpillar and was busy poking at it with a twig. Something had to be done.

Back on board, Nina was yelling, "Quick! Get him! He'll drown!" But Joshy wouldn't be got. So Ned did the only thing possible and announced that they had already landed.

At first they explored the island. Ned fought off and harpooned a crocodile. Nina spotted and harpooned a cucumber. Tinker was stretching in the sun. Ned said it was a man-eating tiger and told Nina to stop tickling its stomach. Then they met the island people. That was when things started going wrong. Ned said they looked frightening. Nina said she liked them and wanted to invite them for dinner.

"But they might attack us!" Ned protested.

"Don't be silly!" she shouted.

"Look! They're coming!"

"I don't care!"

There were tears, red faces, screams. By the time

they had finished, the islanders had gone away. And anyway, it was time for lunch.

"Are we going to get the treasure now?" Nina asked when they went out again.

But Ned was tired of pretending. He could pretend the ship, he could pretend the island, even the islanders and the crocodile, but he wasn't going to pretend the treasure.

"What can we use?" he asked.

"A stone," Nina suggested.

"No. It's got to be something precious."

"I know," said Nina. "Rag Dolly!"

Rag Dolly wasn't quite what Ned wanted, but he couldn't think of anything better. So they trooped up the yard, Ned holding Rag Dolly in one hand and a beach spade in the other.

"Now," he said, "do you know what we're going to do with it?"

"She's not an '*it*'!" Nina said, hurrying after him.

"We're going to bury it." But Nina flatly refused to have Rag Dolly put into the ground.

It was no good. He would have to think of something else. So while Nina comforted Rag Dolly, Ned sat down to think.

Treasure was usually silver or gold. Mommy wouldn't let him bury her jewelry. It would be difficult to get the gold-colored knocker off the front door. What else was there? Just then he heard Joshy coming up the slope and an idea flashed through his mind. Joshy stood dazed as the person he had been coming to see dashed past him in the opposite direction.

Seconds later, Ned dashed back up the slope, clutching something in his hand. It was Joshy's silver spoon!

"Poon!" cried Joshy, as he stumbled around the rock garden and along the path. "Poon! Poon!"

Ned had almost finished digging the hole by the time Joshy got there.

"It's all right," Ned assured him. "You'll get it back again. It's the treasure. You're lucky. You've got the most precious thing in the whole house."

"Yes, you're lucky," agreed Nina, holding very tight to Rag Dolly.

Joshy wasn't sure. He watched Ned dig out a few more shovelfuls of dark earth, wrap the spoon up in an oak leaf, and drop it in. It only took a minute to shovel the earth back over it and stamp it down.

"Can I dig it up now?" asked Nina.

"Not yet," said Ned. "We've got to make a treasure map first. You can't find treasure without a map!" And he hurried off for crayons and paper.

This is the map Ned drew.

It took him a very long time to draw it—especially the skull and crossbones, which somehow looked more like a burger and french fries. Nina watched for a while, asking what things were and why he'd put a big kiss next to the cabbages. It wasn't a kiss, he told her; X marked the treasure. But whenever she asked if it was time to dig it up, all he said was that the map wasn't ready yet. Finally she wandered off. Before Ned had finished, Mom brought out a picnic dinner of sandwiches and cookies on a tray. And then it was bathtime.

The next day they were all up early. Joshy was the

first outside, pulling along his wooden duck. Ned was putting the finishing touches on the treasure map before breakfast when Nina came bursting in in a panic.

"Ned! It's not there! Somebody's digged it up! Come and see!"

They ran through the yard together. Nina was right. The earth had been scooped out again. In the bottom of the hole lay the limp oak leaf, in pieces.

"We must tell Mommy somebody's stolen the treasure," said Nina. Suddenly Ned felt frightened. Joshy's spoon was real silver. Mommy would be angry. "No, don't tell Mommy," he said to Nina. "It must be one-eyed Jake who took it. The horriblest pirate who sails the seas. If you tell on him, Nina, he'll make you walk the plank!"

"Which plank?" said Nina, scared of the way Ned was glaring at her. But there was no time to explain.

"Come on!" called Ned, rummaging under the rhubarb leaves. "Help look for it! We've got to find it!"

At that moment they were called in for breakfast. Ned wished he had never suggested playing pirates!

Why hadn't they buried Rag Dolly instead? He felt hot with shame and worry. Joshy was already at the table when he walked in. Ned sat down and poured out his cereal without speaking. He was terrified that Nina might say something.

Joshy didn't seem bothered. He was dropping bits of chewed toast on the floor. In the end Ned decided he couldn't stand it. It would have been all right if only *he* had to keep the secret, but with Nina and Joshy knowing as well, he felt frightened each time either of them started to speak. There was nothing else to do: he'd have to confess.

"Mom," he began. "You know yesterday. Well, the thing is, we were being pirates and, well, we needed something to bury you see, and—"

"Me found it! Me found it!" shouted Joshy, and in a shower of dirt he pulled the silver spoon out of his front pocket and held it in the air over his head.

"—and Joshy found it again," said Ned, with a relief that nobody else knew. "Isn't he smart!"

Hide and Seek

The leaves were beginning to fall. Ned scuffed his feet through them as he wandered down from the chicken run. There was no point in looking for Tinker any longer. He would have come back by now if he was all right. Ned thrust his hands into his pockets. In one was a chestnut he'd found the day before. He looked it over thoughtfully. They didn't keep their shine for long.

Nina appeared from behind the stone wall, followed by Joshy. She was wearing a pink summer dress and red rubber boots.

"Well, he's not in the vegetable garden," she said.

"He's not by the chicken run either," said Ned. "I've looked in every nook and cranny."

"Tinker dead," said Joshy importantly.

It had happened two days ago, before the children were awake. A man had knocked at the door to ask if a small tabby cat belonged to them. He'd hit it with his van, he said. He'd stopped and walked back to where it was lying on the road, but as he'd gotten near, it had sprung up and run into the bushes and disappeared. He said he was terribly sorry.

Since then Tinker hadn't been seen. They'd called him. They'd looked for him. That was the day before yesterday and there was still no sign of him. Mom and Dad had broken it to them this morning that Tinker had probably died. Cats like to die in private, they'd said. They hide away if they're hurt. But when the children had gone out to play that morning, they'd ended up looking for Tinker again—just one last time, just in case.

Now they stood together glumly under the apple tree.

"Come on," said Ned. "Let's play a game."

"Hiding squeak!" said Joshy.

A moment later, the game had started.

"Where's Joshy?" asked Ned.

"Where's Joshy?" echoed Nina.

In fact, they both knew exactly where Joshy was. He was standing right in front of them with his eyes screwed up and his hands over his face. This, he believed, meant that they couldn't see him. And since everyone enjoyed playing along with it, and leaped with shock or cried, "There he is!" when he opened his eyes again, it was hardly surprising that he continued to believe it.

Ned and Nina thought that if they let Joshy have his turn first, then they could play real hide and seek. But they were wrong.

"Again!" said Joshy.

They soon realized that, given the chance, Joshy would happily go on playing his way until lunchtime.

"It's my turn to hide now," Nina told him. "Cover your eyes while Ned counts to twenty."

All of a sudden Joshy didn't want to cover his eyes any more. "Me hide!" he bawled.

It was so unfair, Nina thought, that little kids could get their way by crying. Reluctantly, she took his hand and set off toward the chicken run while Ned, with his hands over his eyes, counted slowly and loudly toward twenty. They had gotten as far as the holly bush and Ned had gotten to twelve, when Joshy started singing.

"Sh!" said Nina, angrily pressing a finger to her lips. Hardly knowing what was happening to him, Joshy was bustled behind the holly bush and then dragged stumbling over the low branches of the rhododendron den. As Ned called, "Coming," Nina clapped her hand over Joshy's mouth. "Keep quiet!" she whispered fiercely in his ear. Surprisingly, Joshy did as he was told. It didn't take Ned long to find them—Nina usually hid in the rhododendrons. In any case, being found was the part Nina liked best.

"Now it's my turn," said Ned.

"Well, you're taking Joshy with you," said Nina.

"I can't," said Ned. "He wouldn't be able to get to the place where I want to hide."

"Why, where is it?" Nina asked.

"I'm not *telling* you!" said Ned.

"*I* know," said Nina. "You and me can hide and Joshy can look for us." It wasn't what Ned had wanted, but it was better than trying to hide with Joshy—for hiding was the part Ned liked best. But even as they led Joshy into the middle of the lawn, they came upon their first problem.

"Joshy can't count," said Nina.

After a moment's thought, Ned announced that *he* would count—quietly to himself—and then call, "Ready," when they were hidden. The plan was explained to Joshy, who was now sitting on the grass. He held an acorn cup in one hand, while with the other, over and over again, he put the acorn in and took it out. Ned began to get grumpy when it was obvious that Joshy wasn't listening at all. Then he had a good idea.

"I'll give you a chestnut," he said, "if you try and find us."

He took out of his pocket the nice chestnut with

one flat side. Joshy agreed and eventually they got
him to cover his eyes. Ned crept away, leading Nina
after him. Just as they reached the swing, Ned looked
around. There sat Joshy, his acorn in one hand, its
cup in the other, cheerfully watching them go.

It was no good: they'd have to put him somewhere
from which he couldn't watch. Joshy was steered back
into the rhododendron den and forced, much against
his will, to sit down. Ned and Nina made a dash for it.
They reached the apple tree.

"Quick! Up here!" whispered Ned, clambering up
like a monkey. "Come on! He'll *see* you!"

Nina, who'd had no idea she was going to be asked
to hide up a tree, scowled up at him as he anxiously
hissed down advice about where she should put her
feet or hands. But he needn't have worried. Even when
they'd been sitting up in the branches for several minutes, there was still no sign of Joshy.

"Ready!" Ned called for the third time.

"Come and look for us!" Nina yelled.

"Sh!" said Ned, with a frown.

At last, through a gap between the leaves, they saw Joshy emerge from behind the holly bush. He didn't look as if he was searching for anybody, but Nina and Ned exchanged secretive smiles all the same. The minutes went by. They heard the swing creaking.

"Poor old Tinker," Ned sighed. "He used to come up here sometimes."

"Can you think when you're dead?" asked Nina, rather loudly.

"Of course you can't," whispered Ned.

"What *can* you do?"

"You can't do anything."

"Till you come alive again," Nina reminded him.

"You can't come alive again," said Ned.

Just then Joshy appeared beneath them. He stopped, picked up a fallen apple, took a bite out of it, and sat down on the grass. Nina held her hand over her mouth to stifle a giggle. For a while they watched him. He bit into another rosy windfall apple and found a maggot.

Then he picked up another one and tried that. He was soon surrounded by apples with Joshy-sized bites out of them.

All at once Nina blurted out, "What about ghosts?"

Joshy looked up and the game was over.

Next it was Ned's turn on his own. Nina knelt among the apples with Joshy and peeped between her fingers, counting aloud while Ned ran toward the chicken run.

". . . eleven, twelve, fourteen, fifteen, seventeen, sixteen, nineteen, twenty! Come on, Joshy. Let's find Ned and you can have his chestnut." They set off in the direction Ned had taken, but before they even reached the chicken run Ned appeared with a look of sheer astonishment on his face.

"I've just seen Tinker," he said, his mouth hanging open. Nina and Joshy ran to look for him, while Ned hurried to tell Mom. But after they'd all spent a quarter of an hour searching and calling his name without any luck, they were forced to believe that Mom was right and that it couldn't have been Tinker after all.

"Me hide!" said Joshy. But Ned and Nina weren't in the mood now. They felt puzzled and disappointed and hardly noticed Joshy heading off up the garden. Ned poked at the fallen apples wondering if there were such things as cat ghosts. Nina leaned against the tree trunk, sucking her fingers and trying to imagine what it would be like to be a ghost and not be able to think.

Before long they were called in for lunch.

"Where's Joshy?" asked Mom.

Ned vaguely remembered his going off to hide.

"I know where he'll be," said Nina. She ran up to the rhododendron den but came back without him.

"If we call him, he's bound to answer," said Ned. So they all called him, but no answer came.

Ned and Nina set off again through the yard to find Joshy. They looked in the shed, they looked in the woodpile, they looked behind bushes and along the bank, calling him all the time. The only place they had still to look was the chicken run. Nina followed Ned in through the wire-mesh gate. It was obvious that

Joshy wasn't there. The hens were busy scratching in the earth; there was no commotion.

"Let's see if there are any eggs," said Nina as Ned turned to go. She swung open the door of the chicken house. Four eggs sat neatly on the straw of the nesting box. But suddenly, as Nina leaned in to get them, her heart jumped. She gave a loud gasp.

"What is it?" asked Ned.

There, lying in the corner of the chicken house with his legs stuck out in front of him, fast asleep on the warm wood shavings, was Joshy. And draped over his lap, fast asleep too, lay Tinker. Joshy didn't know what was happening when their shouts of joy woke him up.

Maybe he wasn't much good at hide and seek, but Ned and Nina both agreed that finding Joshy was the best part of that whole day.

Spider Pie

"Come and look at the rainbow!" shouted Nina. But by the time Joshy got up the slope it had vanished. "Never mind," she told him, "there might be another one." It was true; Nina had already seen two rainbows that day. The weather was behaving very strangely. Huge woolly clouds would go racing across the sky, then the sun would stream through a patch of bright blue, then moments later a heavy, gray curtain would draw across it and down would come the rain.

"Quick, into the shed! Here comes the rain again!" said Nina.

She and Joshy stood just inside the doorway of the shed while the rain rattled on the roof and window and unlocked all the hidden smells of the earth. Nina deliberately allowed the rain to speckle the toes of her boots: it made her feel how dry the rest of her was.

"Rain," said Joshy, holding his pink hand out into it. "No rainbow. Rain."

When the rain had almost stopped, Acorn came bounding across the lawn and barged into the shed, almost knocking Joshy off his feet as he reached out to pat her. Soon afterward Mom arrived. She'd come to chose some apples from the apple bin in the shed to put into a pie. Nina went back down with her to the house. But Joshy wanted to stay in the shed and play. Acorn

stayed with him, flopping down onto an old sack in the corner.

Joshy loved the shed. It was full of interesting things: there was the lawn-mower; there were stakes which rattled together, stacks of different-sized flower pots, little pointed labels with writing on them, shovels and pitchforks and hoes, and scraps of green netting. But today Joshy had found some empty jars to play with. What's more, in the bottom of them were one, two, three—a whole collection of dried-up spiders!

Joshy examined the spiders in the jar, then tipped them out into a box. Their legs were all curled up around them and some of them were stuck together with cobwebs. Carefully, he disentangled them, picked them up, rolled them between his fingers, sniffed them, and then pretended to run a store with them, while the rain poured down outside. Now and then, Acorn re-arranged herself in the corner with a sigh.

While Joshy played in the shed, Ned and Nina were busy baking in the warm, steamed-up kitchen. Mom had made an apple and blackberry pie with an apple and leaves cut out of pastry on the top of it. She'd given the two of them some pastry to make small pies of their own, with a choice of jam, raisins, or apples to put in them.

"Ned, I can't cut it right," said Nina. "Help me."

"Oh, now it's rolled too thin," she said a moment later. "*You* do it."

"How many hands do you think I have?" asked Ned.

"Not enough," Nina muttered.

Just then, Mom remembered Joshy and the dog and sent Ned out to the shed to get them. He found Joshy busy with something or other in a box.

"Mom says it's time to come in now," said Ned.

"No," said Joshy without turning around.

"But it'll rain again soon and then you won't be able to."

"No," Joshy repeated.

"We're making pies!" said Ned. "You can have some pastry and make some too if you like."

"Me make pies," said Joshy as if he hadn't changed his mind at all. But he wouldn't come right in. He insisted on collecting together some of his bits and pieces to bring down with him. Ned gazed up at the weather while he waited. He watched a small pool of blue being swept across the sky by the hurrying clouds.

"No rainbow," said Joshy as he stepped out of the doorway with an armful of old jars. When they got down to the house, Ned persuaded him to leave them just inside the back door.

"Have you washed your hands?" Mom asked Joshy, who had begun prodding the dough with his fingers.

While Joshy tried to cut out his pastry, the others put the fillings in their pies. Ned chose apples and raisins. Nina chose raisins and jam, but then she added some apples anyway before she put on the tops. Then she helped Joshy who, what with spilling flour all over his lap and getting pastry stuck to his sleeves, was making quite a mess. She offered to put in his fillings for him too, but he wanted to do that himself.

So Ned and Nina left him and pulled a chair up to the sink to do the dishes. Once, while she was picking the sticky dough out of the bristles of the scrub brush, Nina noticed Joshy wandering out to the back door. Perhaps he's lost interest, she thought, seeing that his pies still didn't have their tops on. But he came back again carrying something, and by the time Nina and Ned had dried their hands, Joshy's two pies were ready.

"Mmm, they look delicious," Mom said as she transferred them onto the tray.

The inviting smell of her big pie wafted out of the

oven as she opened it to slide all theirs in underneath. Joshy had his hands and face washed, and Acorn licked up all the bits of pastry dropped under the table. Then they all went outside to play while their pies were baking.

Another downpour had just come and gone, and the leaves were still dripping onto the drenched grass. A hundred shining droplets hanging on the clothesline leaped off when Ned hit it with a stick. For Joshy the yard was a paradise of puddles. He stamped in all of them and even sat down in one. Acorn raced around in circles, barking, then shot off toward the house.

"Did you put jam in your pies, Joshy?" asked Nina.

"No," said Joshy.

"Raisins?" she guessed.

"Piders," said Joshy. "Not raisins. Piders."

Nina made a face and laughed. Ned came over, waving a wet branch like a banner in the air.

"Joshy," said Nina, "tell Ned what you put in your pies."

"Piders," Joshy repeated obediently.

Nina turned to Ned, expecting him to laugh. But he didn't. Instead he just paused for a moment, said, "Oh no!" then dashed down to the house. At the back door he kicked off his boots. When Nina and Joshy arrived he stuck out his head and asked Nina, rather urgently, "Do you know what your pies looked like?"

"Course I do," said Nina.

"No, I mean, *exactly* what they looked like. Or where they were on the tray?"

There was a moment's silence.

"Why?" she asked. But to Ned that silence obviously meant that the answer was no. He picked up one of the jars near the door and asked, "What was in here, Joshy?"

"Piders!" said Joshy with a big smile now that someone at last seemed to understand. "Not now," he added, shaking his head. "Piders all gone."

Nina's mouth fell open.

"Quick!" said Ned. "Let's see if the pies are out of the oven yet."

Nina kicked off her boots and followed him into the

kitchen. They were both too worried to enjoy the delicious smell of baking. There, on a rack in the middle of of the table, were the finished pies. Ned and Nina immediately tried to identify which were theirs. It wasn't as easy as they'd hoped, since some had swollen, some had cracked or collapsed, and nearly all of them had leaked.

"That one's yours," said Ned, "because it had that funny lump on it." Nina didn't much like her decoration being called a "funny lump," but right now there were more important things to worry about. They decided which were hers—the burned trickles of jam helped—but as Ned gathered together his, the horrible truth hit them: both of Joshy's pies were missing!

Joshy, who had been struggling to hang his coat on a hook, arrived just in time to hear the news. The corners of his mouth went down and he blinked, looking from one to the other of them, uncertain whether to yell or cry.

"Mom must have eaten them!" said Nina. "She said

how delicious they looked when she was putting them in the oven. Remember?"

A wail broke from Joshy. But no sooner had his mouth opened than one of Ned's pies was thrust into it.

"Here you are," said Ned, "have one of mine."

"And one of mine," said Nina, while he was still spluttering out crumbs.

The last thing they wanted was for Mom to come and ask what was happening and for Joshy to give the whole thing away. When she did come in a moment later, Joshy had quieted down and was munching alternate mouthfuls of Ned's and Nina's pies with a hurt look on his face.

"Haven't you tried yours yet?" Mom asked them. "They look lovely." Nina and Ned each picked up one of their own pies and sheepishly bit into it.

It was a while before Nina glanced down at hers. There, in the filling, was a small, black, shriveled-up object—she let out a shriek and dropped the pie on the floor. She realized right away what she'd done and tried to pretend that she'd bitten her tongue. But by then it was too late: Joshy had spotted in Nina's splattered pie what were, in fact, only baked raisins and, pointing at it angrily, he shouted. "That my pie! That my pie!"

"No, listen to me," said Mom soothingly, lifting him up.

Oh no, thought Ned and Nina. What's she going to tell him? And *worse*, what will Joshy tell her?

"While you were all outside . . ." she began.

"My piders!" sulked Joshy.

But Mom took no notice and went on: ". . . I'm afraid Acorn jumped up and stole a couple of pies off the rack." Joshy wriggled out of her arms, jumped down, and ran across to Acorn.

"Naughty dog!" he said and gave her as hard a smack as he could on her back. Acorn only wagged her tail. And Ned and Nina gave each other a look that meant "Thank goodness!"

The Castle

At last, after three days, the rain had stopped. Ned, Nina, and Joshy got into their rubber boots and set out for the stream. Acorn had to stay indoors. If she went with them to the stream she'd get filthy and make muddy pawmarks all over the kitchen floor. No sooner were they in the yard than Nina slipped over on the wet grass.

"Don't laugh!" she told Ned, who seemed to think that having a wet rear end was the funniest thing in the world.

Now they had the problem of getting Joshy up the steep bank behind the chicken house. They tried pulling, then they tried pushing, but all they succeeded in doing was smearing a large amount of mud all over him from his nose to his knees. Ned stood at the top of the bank and looked down at him with a sigh. Having to take Joshy with them on expeditions really did make life very difficult. But eventually, after a lot more puffing and shouting. Joshy arrived in a heap at the top.

Along the bank, through the gate, and they'd be there. It sounded easy, but if there was a root to trip over, Joshy would, and if there was a thorn bush around, Nina would get caught on it. Ned was kept busy, picking up one and disentangling the other. But in the end they reached the wooden gate to the field. Ned climbed over and the other two climbed through —all at the same time. So that Ned stood on Nina's fingers and she and Joshy banged their heads together.

It might have been enough to spoil the whole expedition if they hadn't just then heard the rushing water for the first time.

The days of rain had swelled the little stream. Where it flowed in a channel it was much deeper than usual —as Joshy quickly proved by filling one boot with water. Where the banks were low it was much wider than usual—as Joshy proved by leaving the other boot stuck in the middle of it.

It was in this part of the stream that Nina found her castle. A knot of old tree stumps with their roots showing stuck up out of the mud, while the stream divided in two and flowed around each side of them. There were several small ledges at different heights—just right for rooms—and in one stump there was even a round hollow full of water for a sink. While Joshy was seeing how much mud he could squeeze out between his fingers, and Ned was trying—rather unsuccessfully— to sail twigs down the stream, Nina decided which room was which. The first Ned knew of her castle was when she called out to him, "Dinner's ready!"

Ned stepped over the stream and sat down on part of the stump.

"Not there!" she said. "You don't have dinner in the bathroom!"

He did what he was told, although the dining room had a rather nasty spike sticking out of it and he would have been more comfortable where he was.

"Joshy!" called Nina. "How many times do I have to tell you dinner's ready?"

Joshy had to be helped up and was wedged between two stumps where he wouldn't fall out. Dinner was moss and beechnuts, two leaves each, and an imaginary cup of tea. Ned said it was very nice and politely dropped it in the stream. Joshy didn't say anything, but would have given it a try if they hadn't stopped him just in time.

"Would you like a moat, Nina?" Ned asked casually.

"Can you eat it?" said Nina.

"Me want one!" said Joshy, picking moss out of his mouth.

"No, a moat," explained Ned, "is when you have water all around your castle so enemies can't get you."

Nina thought about it while a sparrow cheeped nearby. "What if they've got boats?"

"You just drop rocks on them or pour boiling oil over them."

"All right," said Nina, "but *I've* got my own work to do."

So Ned explained his plan to Joshy. "What we have to do is dam up the stream with stones and mud and things, then the water will—"

But Joshy didn't wait to hear the rest of the plan. In no time he was back with his first armful of dirt. Splosh! it went, into the stream, splattering everyone, and was immediately washed away. Ned decided they would first have to make a wall of stones across the stream, then fill it in with grass and dirt afterward. While Ned grunted and strained to dig up a larger boulder, Joshy set off across the field and came back with a pebble no bigger than an egg. He then stood on the edge of the stream and threw it in his stiff-armed way at the water.

"Ouch! What was that?" shouted Nina, putting her hand to her neck. Throwing wasn't Joshy's strong point.

A few minutes later Joshy came back with something else. "Look Ned! Look Nina!" he called waving a large bone in the air.

"That's probably from a dinosaur," said Ned, looking up from the boulder he had now rolled as far as the stream. Joshy didn't know what a dinosaur was but he guessed it was something good. He was feeling rather proud of himself, when Ned snatched it out of his hand, saying, "Just what we need," and rammed it into the middle of the stream. After that Joshy didn't feel much like helping. But Ned kept on working hard and soon the stream was completely blocked by a wide dam as high as his knee.

"There!" said Ned, stepping across the already deeper water onto Nina's castle.

"Wipe your feet!" said Nina.

A moment later the sun came out. Ned sat with his chin on his knees, feeling very pleased with himself as the water level rose behind the dam. He gazed at the tiny things floating in it as the sun warmed his back, while Nina chattered away about this and that; he said just enough to make her think he was listening. Time slowed down. The water, too, gradually stopped moving. A wren was busy in the bank, making that sound like an old clock being wound up.

Suddenly Ned looked around. The moat! Nina's castle now had a deep pond all the way around it. They were completely cut off! How would they get back? They couldn't possibly step over it or even jump!

"Help!" he wailed. "The water! We're stuck!"

Nina looked one way, then the other, then at Ned, and burst into tears. "*You* did it!" she sobbed. "I didn't want a moat anyway!"

Ned shouted frantically for Joshy, who was sitting some way off, trying to dry out his boot with a handful

of grass. He half put it on and came stumbling over
to the stream. For a moment he just stood looking at
them as if to say, "What a silly thing to be doing."

"Quick!" began Ned. "Go and—" But just then
Nina held up her chin, opened her mouth like a sea-
gull on a rooftop, and let out a blood-curdling scream.

"Go and get Mommy!" Ned tried again.

"Can't get my boot on," said Joshy. "You help."

"How can I help!" shouted Ned, waving his hands
in the air. "I'm stuck! Go on Joshy! Go and get her!
Or we'll be drowned and you'll never see us again!"

Joshy thought for a while, but in the end he hobbled off to do as he was told. They saw him leaning back through the gate to pick up his boot. They watched him make his way—so slowly, it seemed—along the bank. Then all at once, like a rabbit going down its hole, he disappeared.

The two of them waited. Ned looked grimly at the water. It seemed to be rising every second. Nina looked grimly at Ned, whose stupid fault it all was. When their eyes met, Ned stared down at her feet in shame.

"You have your boots on the wrong feet," he told her solemnly.

"Don't be silly!" she snapped. "I don't have any other feet."

They seemed to wait an awfully long time. Then suddenly there was a crackling and rustling and Acorn came blundering into the field.

"Oh no!" Ned cried. "He's let Acorn out. We'll be in trouble now."

Acorn made straight for the moat and leaped in. For a little while she frolicked in the muddy pond,

showering them with water each time she shook
herself. Then all at once she took an interest in the
dam. At first it was just her nose she poked into it,
then she started scrabbling at the earth with her front
paws.

Before Nina and Ned realized what was happening,
she had scooped a big hole in the dam and the water
had started pouring through it. She carried on, scratching away more and more until the water whooshed
past her. Good old Acorn! The pond level was going
down fast. Nina let out a sort of sobbing laugh. But
still Acorn was burrowing away. She stood now in
shallow mud, with her wet fur sticking to her body.

Then with a jerk of her head she tugged out . . . that bone!

Ned and Nina climbed down from the tree root and patted her. They both laughed. It didn't seem now as if they'd been in much danger at all. But then they noticed each other's clothes: covered in dirt and soaking wet. What would Mommy say? Suddenly Joshy arrived, shouting about Acorn.

"Have you told Mommy?" Ned asked anxiously.

"No," said Joshy. "Acorn got out . . ."

"Well, you mustn't tell," said Ned.

"If you don't," began Nina, wondering what she could promise—"if you don't, Joshy, if you *don't* tell tell Mommy . . . you can have your bone back!" This seemed fair to Joshy, who, in any case, couldn't see any point in telling now that they were safe.

As they made their way home Ned whispered to Nina, "Remember, don't say anything about the castle."

"No," Nina agreed. "Only, we'd better tell Mommy that it was Joshy who let Acorn out. Don't you think?"

Halloween

It was the day of Halloween, when all the children in the town dressed up as ghosts or witches or monsters and went along to the town hall after dark for a just-a-little-bit scary party. Ned and Nina each had a witch's hat. Ned's had silver stars and moons on it and Nina's had wispy green hair that hung down at the back from inside the rim. The problem was, what could Joshy go as? They thought about it as they tried to get the rest of their costumes together.

"He's too small for a monster," said Nina.

"What else is scary?" said Ned, rummaging through the dress-up box for something black.

"I know. Spiders," said Nina.

Ned thought. "But how could we make him look like a spider? He doesn't have enough legs."

At this point Joshy, who had been happily reading an upside-down book in the armchair, came running across to join Ned at the dress-up box. Joshy didn't dress up *as* things—he just dressed up. And since he couldn't yet dress himself in his *own* clothes, and since most of the clothes in the box were far too big for him anyway, he usually ended up looking like nothing more than a walking clothes heap. On this occasion, however, Joshy knew exactly what he wanted to wear. He stood, pointing up at Nina, and proclaimed, "Me hat! Me hat!"

"It's too big for you, Joshy," said Nina.

But Joshy just repeated his demand louder than ever, with a face that threatened to crumple into tears and screaming, for which Nina knew she'd be blamed. Unhooking the elastic from under her chin, she thrust the hat at him, muttering that she'd put a spell on him when she got it back. Joshy went blundering off, with the hat on backward down over his eyes, so that the green hair got in his mouth each time he opened it to make cackling noises.

"Look," called Ned. He held up a ragged piece of black material that had once been the lining of a raincoat. "This would work as a cape for you."

"It's horrible," Nina said, catching sight of the black velvet skirt that now hung on Ned's back, fastened with a brooch under his chin.

"But witches are meant to be horrible."

"Well, aren't wizards?" Nina burst out. "Why should you have that nice cape and not me?"

But Ned had an answer. "Wizards stay in their caves

inventing spells and writing them in books, but witches go out at night doing horrible, nasty things and riding around on their broomsticks. Anyway, don't you want to win the prize?" he asked her.

"What prize?"

"The prize for the most frightening person there."

"All right," agreed Nina. "But I get the broomstick!" And with that she left the room.

In a moment she was back, looking angrier than ever.

"It's the wrong kind!" she said.

Ned tried to hide a grin. He'd known that all along, she could tell. There he stood, in his hat, with a real cape—and now he'd even found himself a wand! And what did she have? Nothing! It wasn't fair.

"What else do witches have?" said Nina angrily.

"A cat," said Ned with an unhelpful shrug.

And it was at that moment, as if by magic, that Nina had her idea. "That's what Joshy can go as: a witch's cat!"

Everything went well after that. Nina settled for

a ragged cape and Mom found her a pair of black tights with holes in them and an old pair of Ned's black sneakers. Then Ned helped her make a cat outfit for Joshy. In the dress-up box there was a gray fur jacket with the sleeves missing that would nearly come down to his knees. They got an old tiger mask, painted it black, and fixed the elastic. Then they secretly snapped off a handful of bristles from the stiff broom that was the wrong kind for flying on, and taped them to the mask for whiskers. Finally, Ned got his woolly blue bathrobe belt, to be poked into Joshy's pants as a tail. With the plan complete, they set about painting their own faces to make them look as gruesome as possible.

As it began to grow dark, the children grew more and more excited. Even Joshy was excited, though he had no idea what was going on. He did a little dance as if he were trying to stamp out a fire, and let out a kind of strangled yell. Nina and Ned, already in their costumes, waited for him to calm down so that they could dress him up in his.

But it was when he calmed down that the trouble started. No one had actually *asked* Joshy whether he wanted to be a cat. They put his arms through the sleeve holes of the fur coat—he pulled them out. They poked in his tail—he tore it away. They fitted the mask over his face—he snatched it off, snapping the elastic, and flung it stubbornly to the ground.

Ned looked at Nina anxiously. Would this be the signal for another fit of tears?

But Nina was too excited to let that upset her. "Joshy can go as Joshy," she said.

It was time to leave. Night had fallen. They felt their eyes open wide like owls as they stepped out into the darkness. But there was a bright half-moon which cast jagged shadows at their feet and made Nina's face look more witchy and hideous than ever.

"You three walk together and I'll follow behind," said Mom.

As they hurried along the lane holding hands, the black shapes of trees and bushes shifted spookily all around them.

"Dark!" said Joshy, again and again.

"Are there ghosts out now?" Nina wanted to know.

"Not really," Ned answered, but he walked on the other side of the road as they passed the empty house just in case a ghost jumped out at him.

"Moon!" Joshy told them for the tenth time.

Ned made a laughing noise. If the truth were known, Ned was more nervous than any of them about the horrible things that Halloween might bring out. It was good to have a fearless Joshy to hold on to.

Nina felt her heart pounding as they opened the door of the town hall. There, in the dim red and green light, a host of other Halloween creatures cavorted to the sound of ghostly music. Nina hadn't forgotten the prize. She felt overwhelmed and disappointed at first to see so many witches with things she hadn't thought of, like a pointed nose, a hat with cobwebs, or long, twisted fingernails. Enviously, she eyed one who even had a witch's broom. But when a bat in ballet shoes who came flapping up to her turned out to be her friend Sarah, she ran off happily enough to join in the haunting.

Ned stayed on the sidelines and walked quietly along the edge of the room, casting spells with an elaborate wave of his wand.

As for Joshy, he ran around laughing, bumping into ghouls and gremlins, blissfully unaware that he looked no more ghostly than on any other day of the year.

After a number of games, accompanied by a lot of giggling and squealing, everyone sat down for the refreshments. The feast was spread on a row of trestle tables draped with long white tablecloths. The hot dogs were labeled dead man's fingers, the ketchup was called blood sauce, and there were nasty names for everything else, from the green gelatin mold to the chocolate pudding.

Joshy enjoyed himself as much as anybody, taking a mouthful of chips followed by a mouthful of pudding, a bite of hot dog followed by one of cake. He was one of the last ones left at the table and had just climbed down to get a chocolate cookie that had rolled off his plate when Mr. Bryers, the grown-up in charge, spoke.

"If all you children would come away from the tables now while we clear away the food, we'll put all the lights out except for this candle and we'll decide which of you here is the horriblest sight. I don't want anyone being silly, but the one who frightens me most will win the Halloween prize."

With that he lit a thick church candle that stood on a shelf and the lights went off. The children began milling around in the flickering candlelight. There was growling, muttering, cackling, hooting, groaning, wailing, and, of course, plenty of giggling. One girl burst into tears, but not from fright—one of the tiniest witches' hats had poked her in the eye.

Mr. Bryers stooped in the middle of the moving crowd, squinting doubtfully at the faces that came past him—Nina's, it seemed, more often than most. Then suddenly, in the darkness behind him, there was a colossal crash! At the same moment, with a piercing scream, a ghostly white shape covered in ghastly stains came groping toward them. Children of all ages shrieked and went running to the other end of the hall. Mr. Bryers himself had nearly jumped out of his skin and could still barely make out in the dimness what it was—this screeching apparition, almost too small to be human, that no one had seen before.

The lights came on. There were sighs of relief, then puzzlement, then laughter. Joshy had climbed under the table to get his chocolate cookie back and had discovered all kinds of other dropped goodies down there. In fact, he was still sitting among them when suddenly the lights had gone out. He waited for a moment while he finished what was in his mouth, then stood up in the pitch darkness and walked forward.

He grabbed hold of the hanging tablecloth as it

wrapped itself over his face, but it wasn't till he dragged it right off the table and the last dishes and bowls went clattering onto the floor around him, that he let out his blood-curdling scream. And so he had staggered on, screaming for help, without the faintest idea what was happening to him, until the lights went on and a laughing Mr. Bryers lifted the damp dirty tablecloth from his head.

After that the party was soon over. When Dad arrived to collect the three of them, Joshy held out a box of liquorice candies toward him.

"What's this?" Dad asked.

"It's all right," said Ned, "he's going to share them." And both he and Nina began telling him at the same time what had happened. How proud the witch and the wizard were now of their little brother. And how surprised their father was that it was Joshy, who'd gone dressed up as nothing at all, who had won the Halloween prize!

A Change in the Weather

Nina sat at the window, watching all the big, beautiful flakes of snow disappearing as they touched the ground. Ned came into sight, throwing a glider he had made. Nina decided to go out and play with him.

"Watch out!" called Ned, as she appeared in her striped ski cap, gloves, and scarf. "Flight three-one-four's coming in to land." The glider swooped down

and crashed into a bush. Very carefully Ned disentangled it, then went back into the middle of the lawn to try again. Nina bent down, scraped a little pile of frost from a blade of grass and put it on her tongue.

"What does it taste like?" asked Ned.

"Wonderful," said Nina.

Ned interrupted his flying to try some.

"It's just like water," he said.

"Well, water's wonderful, isn't it!" said Nina. She watched Ned for a little longer before asking, "Can I try?"

"No, sorry," said Ned. "It might break."

"It might break when *you* do it!"

"Yes, but *I* made it. So if I break it, that's my fault, and I don't have to be angry with anyone else."

Nina thought about this for a minute. She sank her mouth into the coils of her scarf, enjoying the moist, woolly warmth of her own breath. She looked up again as the glider looped over and nose-dived straight into the stone wall.

"Is it broken?" she called as Ned knelt to examine it.

"No," said Ned.

"Well then," she said, "I can try it. *I* won't throw it at the wall."

Grumpily, Ned agreed. He didn't know why he was

in such a bad mood. Perhaps it was because after all the hard careful work of following the instructions and fitting everything together, the glider just wouldn't fly straight. Watching Nina trying to throw it like a boomerang didn't help.

"All right," he said when she'd picked it up a third time, "you've had your turn now."

"No-oo," said Nina.

The next time she threw it, Ned raced to get it. A squabble began. At the height of the squabble, a well-wrapped Joshy arrived. No sooner had he seen what the argument was about than he cried, "Me have pane!"

"Now look what you've done!" Ned accused Nina. "Joshy thinks *he* can have it!"

Joshy, who could turn a tantrum on and off like a faucet, immediately joined in at full volume. Fortunately, he couldn't grab the glider, since all his four fingers seemed to be crammed into just two fingers of his gloves. His hat, too, was down over his eyes by the time Mom came out to see what was going on. She crossly told Ned to let each of them have two turns and then it would be time to go out, which was why Joshy had been bundled up in the first place.

It was dark by the time they got home that day, dark and cold, and the sky felt so low it seemed you could have climbed a ladder and touched it. When they woke up the next morning, both Ned and Nina could tell that something had happened, though neither of them knew what until they looked out the window. All night it had been snowing, slowly, steadily, building up this white surprise.

They couldn't wait to get out in it. It didn't seem as cold as yesterday. But the weather wasn't the only thing that changed: Ned was the opposite of the grumpy boy he'd been the day before. He was cheerful and friendly, helpful and kind.

"Look, snow, Joshy! That's snow!" he said, putting his arm around Joshy as he waddled out in his rubber boots, wrapped and padded, to examine this whitened world. Nina went galloping up the path to the lawn.

"Hold on!" called Ned. "Don't walk on it, Nina. It's a shame to spoil it. Let's go into the field and make a snowman, shall we? Come on, Joshy. I'll show you how to do it."

He grabbed Acorn too as she bounded up towards the lawn. "Coming for a walk, Acorn? Good dog, come on!"

Tinker came too, sniffing everywhere, and jumped off the wall in front of them into a drift of snow.

"Where Tinker's legs gone?" said Joshy.

The snow was up to their ankles in the field—in Joshy's case, up to his ankles *inside* his boots. Three steps was the most he took that day without tumbling over, but at least it was soft to fall on. It was good sticking snow as well, perfect for rolling. Ned and Nina tramped up to the top of the field and rolled down a snowball that peeled up all the snow in its path, growing bigger and heavier until they could hardly stop it.

By the time Joshy realized how cold he was and began to whine, the snowman was finished: no arms,

no legs, but the goofiest set of teeth you've ever seen. As they sat indoors having their lunch, it was good to look out and see it standing there so solidly, with that long green strip leading down to it like a carpet rolled out for an important visitor.

Ned continued to be quite unlike himself after lunch

too. "*I* know!" he said. "Let's all do a jigsaw puzzle."
And he went off to get one.

They waited in amazement to see what he'd bring.
Joshy's jigsaws were too easy for Nina and Nina's
were too hard for him. As for Ned's own puzzles, he
generally kept them well away from Joshy. For Joshy's
idea of helping was at best to make a collection of pieces
he wouldn't give back, and at worst to try jamming
them together without paying any attention to the
picture.

So it was a complete surprise when Ned came in
with one of his own favorite jigsaw puzzles and spread
it out on the floor for anyone to grab or trample on.
What had come over him? He would normally have
been the first one back out in the snow. But here he was,
kneeling on the rug, helping Nina to find the straight
edges and offering Joshy pieces for his collection.

This game continued happily until Nina noticed that
it was snowing again. Ned tried to persuade them to
finish the puzzle but when he could see they were deter-
mined to go out, he quickly got dressed too and made

sure that he was the first one in the yard. "Come on,"
he said. "Let's go and see our snowman."

But Nina wanted to go to the rhododendrons. She
wanted to see if it was dry underneath. She wanted to
sit there while it was snowing and feel cozy out of
doors. Joshy followed her up the slope, squeaking with
excitement and flapping his arms and stamping, like
an ostrich trying to take off.

"Poor Daddy!" said Ned just as Nina was about to
walk across the smooth, white lawn. "He won't be able
to take a photo of how beautiful it looks if we walk all
over it, will he?"

Nina didn't want to spoil anything for her dad, so
they turned around and Ned led them into the lower

field. They played there together, making snow pies and cracking the thin ice on the stream, until the snow turned to rain and it started to grow dark.

It must be said that Ned was not quite so helpful at supper and that once he actually got angry in the bath, when Joshy squeezed an ice-cold spongeful of water down his back.

When they woke the next morning, as mysteriously as it had come, all the snow had disappeared. A drab, gray lump of snowman stood at the bottom of the field. Nina felt disappointed. She wished the snow had stayed longer and gotten even deeper. But Ned was remarkably cheerful about it. He was dressed before the others (which was not usual), and was so eager to get outside you'd have thought he hadn't seen wet green grass for years. He was a bit quieter when he came back in again.

After breakfast they all went out to play. Nina watched him for a while prowling around the yard. She could see his bad mood smoldering into life again.

"What's the matter?" she asked.

"I can't find my glider," he told her. "You know, the one you and Joshy had a turn with. I'm sure I left it on the lawn when I went in the other night."

"You did," said Nina timidly. "But I found it."

Ned's temper flared up. "Well, where is it then? It must be somewhere!"

"Is that why you didn't want us to come up here? 'Cause you thought it was under the snow and someone would step on it?"

"No," said Ned. "Yes. Where *is* it?"

Nervously Nina lifted her arm and pointed over the hedge.

"What! In the field?" bellowed Ned. "But we were tramping around in there!"

Nina shook her head and pointed a little higher. "Look. In the tree."

"What tree?" snapped Ned. And then he saw. Lodged in the branches, a good ten paces beyond the remains of their snowman, was his glider. A grin spread across his face.

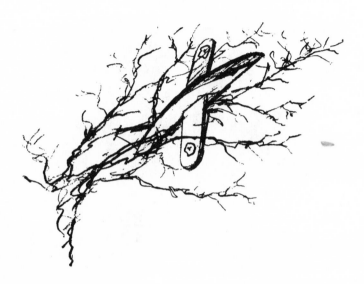

"And it flew all that way by itself?" he said.

Nina nodded. "It's really good. I just took off that plastic piece in the front."

"Come on," said Ned, "let's see if it'll do it again!"

And off they ran together into the field.

Beasty

The grass had been cut for the first time that year and the green, juicy smell of it filled the air. Yet Ned didn't feel like playing outside, with Nina sick in bed. He tried hard to play with Joshy, but carrying stones in a bucket from one side of the garden to the other wasn't all that much fun—even if you were pretending that they were chocolate cakes. After a while he went in to see how Nina was feeling.

The whole room seemed to know she was sick. It smelled different; it looked different with its curtains drawn on the daylight. Ned sat down on the side of the bed and Nina turned over toward him. Her face had no shine, she blinked more slowly than usual, and her voice, when she spoke, seemed to come from farther away.

"Ned," she said, "is it always today?"

"What do you mean?" he asked.

"I mean, is it always today?"

"No. After today there's tomorrow, and then the next day—"

"But what will it be called tomorrow?" she asked him.

"Tomorrow it'll be tomorrow. Wednesday, or Friday, or whatever it is."

"It won't," she said. "It'll be today again."

Ah well, thought Ned. He changed the subject and told her that he'd seen the first robins of the year.

"Just think," he said. "They've flown from somewhere down south all the way back to our house!"

"How do they know the way?" Nina said.

Ned wished she wouldn't keep asking such awkward questions. He'd only come to try and cheer her up. He offered to read her a story but she didn't want one. He offered to get her a drink but she already had one. So he said goodbye and wandered out aimlessly into the yard again.

That evening when he went to bed Nina was already asleep. But in the night he was suddenly woken by her shouting, "Beasty! Beasty!" Ned guessed it was a nightmare and went over to see if she was all right, but she wasn't awake so he left her and went back to bed.

The next morning Ned told her, "You had a bad dream last night. About some monster."

"How do you know what it was about?" asked Nina suspiciously. "Were you in it?"

"No, but I heard you shouting, 'Beasty! Beasty!'"

"Beasty's not a monster. He's my friend," said Nina.

"Your friend?" said Ned with a grin. "Well, why were you frightened then?"

"Maybe someone was going to hurt him," she said as if it were all too obvious.

"And *did* they?" Ned teased.

"Don't remember," she said with a shrug. "It was only a dream."

Ned would have left it at that if she hadn't added, in a terribly matter-of-fact way, "Real Beasty can't get hurt. He's magic."

Now he felt uneasy. Up until then he'd thought Nina was just making up an imaginary friend—this Beasty business. But she seemed quite serious about it. And strangest of all was that she didn't seem to care whether he believed it or not. Of course, he *didn't* believe it. How *could* it be true? All the same, he couldn't help asking what this Beasty looked like.

"He looks nice," Nina told him. Ned had hoped for more than that, but he couldn't really ask any more questions without making her think that he believed in it. He didn't want that.

Nina still wasn't well enough to get up, so after breakfast Ned and Joshy went out to play by themselves again. Ned was surprised how lonely he felt without her. Quite often they played separately, but somehow it was nice having her around. Joshy was absorbed in some game with his red tractor, talking away to himself while he gathered twigs and earth and put them in the trailer. Suddenly Ned had a good idea: he'd pick a few daffodils and take them up for Nina. While he was choosing them, he noticed that several right at the back near the wall had been trampled.

"Did *you* break these flowers?" he asked Joshy sternly.

"Not me," said Joshy, shaking his head, and he drove away.

Nina seemed to be feeling a bit better now and was pleased with the daffodils. Ned suggested playing "I spy." Nina couldn't guess his first word or his second word. But she didn't mind having to give up. Now it was her turn.

"I spy, with my little eye, something beginning with M."

Ned looked around. He could hardly find anything that began with M. He tried mirror, model, mouth. Nina shook her head. "Shall I tell you?"

Ned looked about blankly. "Are you sure it starts with M?" he asked.

"Yes," she laughed. "Give up?"

He nodded.

"Me!" she said.

Ned felt annoyed for a moment, then he remembered how he'd missed her company in the garden. But perhaps it was better to stop playing "I spy" anyway. For a while they talked about television and birds' nests.

Then they fell silent. Ned leafed through a picture book that had been his when he was little. He was surprised to find he knew almost all the words by heart. He'd just put it down and was thinking of going when Nina said, "Do you know?"

"What?" Ned asked.

"Do you *know*?" she said.

Ned knew that he was supposed to say No. Usually she wouldn't go on unless you said No. But he didn't like saying No, when he didn't know what she was talking about. Quite often it turned out to be either something that he did know or something silly that wasn't worth knowing anyway. But you couldn't be sure of that. One thing you *could* be sure of was that if you didn't give the answer she wanted, Nina would get nasty very quickly. So, trying not to sound too interested, Ned said, "No."

"We-ell," Nina began very thoughtfully, "you know Beasty . . ." She waited.

"Yes," said Ned grudgingly. Not Beasty again, he thought, though part of him was curious.

"Well, he thinks you're nice."

"How do you know?"

"He told me when he came to see me this morning."

Ned would have liked to laugh and just walk away. But it was no good: his curiosity was aroused.

"What sort of things does he do, this friend of yours?"

"Well," said Nina, "sometimes he plays in the garden by himself. He *is* a bit clumsy, Beasty is. He steps on the flowers sometimes, by accident." Ned felt a cold shiver run down his back as he remembered the broken daffodils in the garden.

"But how do you know if he's been here?" he asked.

"Sometimes you can see his footprints on the grass,

'cause although he's quite small, he's very heavy—well, heavier than me. Anyway, he leaves messages for me."

"What, writing?" said Ned. It wasn't that he was trying to catch her out. It just suddenly occurred to him that she couldn't read.

"No, he puts down sticks in a special way. Like this, and this," she explained, showing him with her fingers.

"I can't tell you *everything*, 'cause it's Beasty and my's secret." They talked for a while longer, then Ned said he was going downstairs to paint a picture.

"Ned," Nina said, "ask Mommy when she brings my lunch up to bring an extra plate for Beasty, and something for him to drink, will you?"

Ned promised he would. He still wasn't sure whether it was true but he wished *he* had a friend like Nina's that he could talk about and not just be making it up.

Joshy came in while Ned was drawing and joined him at the table, cutting and gluing a complicated mess until lunchtime. Although Mom didn't say anything when she took up Nina's tray, Ned noticed that there was a spare plate on it and two cups of orange juice. That made him wonder again.

But something that happened later that afternoon in the yard positively stopped him in his tracks. He'd been tying a rope from the ash tree to the swing and working on a way to send a flowerpot along it, when all of a sudden he looked down and saw—a mysterious pattern of sticks! At once he remembered what Nina had said about Beasty's messages. Surely there was no way they could have fallen like that by themselves. Somebody, or something, had done it!

Moments later, he noticed a strange hole in the grass —almost round but not quite—and there, not far away from it, was another. Beasty's footprints! Looking around, he discovered yet more. Ned placed his foot on one of them and stretched out his other leg to see if he could reach the next one. Even holding out his arms to help him balance, he nearly toppled over. For the small animal Nina had described, this Beasty took big steps!

He suddenly felt bothered by the thought that Beasty might be watching him, out there on his own. So he abandoned his rope-and-flowerpot machine and went indoors, glad to surround himself with the sounds from the radio and Joshy's chattering.

Nina felt better after dinner and got up for a bath. Should he tell her about the sticks and the footprints? he wondered. He didn't want to sound too serious about it just in *case* it wasn't true, so he decided to wait until she mentioned Beasty herself. But she didn't. She chattered away all right and seemed much more her old self, but not a word was said about her invisible friend. She obviously didn't care whether Ned believed in it or not. In a way, that was the most disturbing part of all.

The next day Nina was back to normal. She got up, ate an enormous breakfast, and went out into the yard with Joshy and Ned. The sun sparkled on the wet grass. And as if to celebrate her recovery, the moon, she noticed, was up there to greet her too. Nina took a deep breath of the sweet-scented air: it seemed like years since she'd been out in the open.

"Nina not sick now," said Joshy solemnly shaking his head, as if just to make sure there hadn't been some mistake.

Ned watched to see whether she'd look around for messages, but instead she went straight to the apple tree. Once she perched up there, she thought, she'd really know she was better. Ned clambered up behind her. It was good to have Nina's company again.

She sat down on her usual branch, with the clear, washed blue of the sky above and the pink-tinged buds of the apple tree all around her. Ned sat down next to her. They smiled at each other.

"Move over," said Nina, "and make some room for Beasty."

Ned thought for a moment. Then he moved along the branch—just in case.